Kieth Allen
August 15, 1948.

Attendance award in
Children's church.
Dare L

WINKY

WINKY
Lost in the Rockies

by

KEN ANDERSON

Author, *Shadows Under the Midnight Sun, The Austin Boys—Marooned!, The Doctor's Return,* etc.

ZONDERVAN PUBLISHING HOUSE
GRAND RAPIDS MICHIGAN

Eight Forty-seven Ottawa Avenue
Grand Rapids, Michigan

CHAPTER 1

Warren Wilcox is his name, but everyone calls him Winky. He got that nickname because of his eyes. Really, his name ought to be Twinkly, instead of Winky, only Winky is much easier to say and to remember than Twinkly. He has the winkiest eyes you ever saw . . . especially when he gets some big idea all his own—like the time last November when he decided to learn to fly with the wings of the Thanksgiving turkey. Boy, he jumped off the garage roof, and if he hadn't landed in the hedge, he might have broken both of his shoestrings; he couldn't make those wings fly a bit! Anyway, whenever he feels especially good or thinks of something extra special, his eyes begin to blink and twinkle.

School was out, and Winky had passed all his subjects . . . even geography and arithmetic. As usual, he planned to spend the summer at the home of his grandparents, Mr. and Mrs. Charley Wilcox, who lived on a small ranch near the Rockies.

Winky had a lot of pals out there: Mike O'Grady and his sister Annie; Donny Sutherland and his sister Lucy; and then, best of all, Bobby Anker, whose father's ranch was across the road from Grandfather's.

Usually, Winky liked to sleep late every morning, and sometimes he barely made it to school in time. But this first morning of vacation he was up as soon as the sun showed its red head. Before the dew was off the grass, he was out pushing the lawn mower.

"Yep, Boston," he said to his little bulldog, "this'll probably be the last time we'll mow the lawn for a few weeks . . . this lawn, anyway. I suppose Grandpa has sheep that graze on his lawn. Hope so, anyway." He swung the machine around the lily pond, frightening one of the gold fish so much that it almost swallowed too much water and got sick. "I ought to get a letter from Grandma in the mail today, Boston."

The dog looked up. Winky thought he was asking, "May I go along?"

"Sure, I guess you can go along, Boston. Only you can't whine in the baggage car all the time like you did last summer. Boy, did I feel silly when the baggage man made me come up and sit with you those last hundred miles on that local out of Denver, because you wouldn't be quiet!"

Boston, as though sorry that he had been scolded, turned to chase a leaf that the wind was blowing across the yard. Winky returned to his mowing.

By breakfast time Winky was hungry enough to eat spinach . . . almost.

Mom smiled at him, "Well, Mother's big man, that was surely nice of you to get up so early and mow the lawn!"

Winky's eyes twinkled. It always made him very happy when Mom said nice things to him. He guessed he had the best mom in the whole world.

"A special delivery letter came this morning just for you!" continued Mom.

"F-For me, Mom? Wh-Who's it from?"

"It's there beside your plate."

When Winky saw that the letter was from Mrs. Charley Wilcox, Foothills, Colorado, he forgot all about the scrambled eggs and even the blackberry jam.

"Oh, boy," he shouted, "it's from Grandma!"

His eager fingers tore it open.

Dear Winky,

Grandfather and I have been so busy with the cattle that I haven't had time to write to you, and because I know you are very anxious, I'm sending this special delivery.

Grandfather wanted me to tell you that we have a very special surprise for you when you come. We can't tell you what it is, because then it wouldn't be a surprise. But I know it is something that will make you very happy. Bobby has seen it, and he thinks it is wonderful. I'm sure this makes you all the more anxious. Bobby promised, though, that he wouldn't write and tell you what it is.

Greet your mother and daddy, Winky. We are very anxious to see you, so come as soon as you can. We pray that God will bless you and give you a safe journey.

Lovingly yours,
GRANDMA

"Boy, oh, boy!" Winky's eyes looked like soap bubbles about to burst. "Is that something, Mom! A surprise! I wonder what it is? Boy, oh, boy!"

Dad came to the table.

"Did you hear the letter, Dad?" Winky asked.

"Yes, I did. That makes you happy, doesn't it?"

"What do you think the surprise is, Dad?"

"Oh, maybe an airplane, or—"

"Aw, not an airplane, do you think?" Winky was very serious.

"Maybe it is a pet eagle that flies," Mom laughed, "and you can ride on its back."

"Aw!" Winky knew now that they were only teasing him and trying to make him wonder all the more.

"Maybe we'd better eat breakfast now," Mom suggested, "and then we can talk things over afterward."

Winky noticed something strange about the way his mother said that, but he didn't say anything.

They all bowed their heads, and Mr. Wilcox asked the blessing on the meal.

Then they ate.

When the meal was over, Dad cleared his throat three

times. Winky knew that meant something important was
coming.

"Winky?"

"Y-Yes."

"Would it disappoint you very much if you didn't get
to go to Grandpa's ranch next week?"

"N-Not . . . g-go, Dad, t-to the ranch?"

"If you had something better?" Mom said hastily.

Something better! As far as Winky knew, there was
no better way in all the world to spend the summer vacation than to go to Grandpa Wilcox's ranch.

"Yes," Dad repeated, "if you had something better?"

"But—" Winky stammered.

"The thing is this, Winky," Dad explained. "Your mother
and I have been thinking of sending you to the Bible camp
for boys and girls which is up on Lake Mirror."

Winky's heart dropped right down into the bottom of
his shoe.

"Now," Dad continued, "this Bible camp is only for
three weeks, Winky, and maybe you could still spend a
couple of weeks at your grandfather's ranch. That would
make a five-week vacation, you see, instead of the usual
four-week vacation."

"I . . . uh . . . uh . . ." For a moment Winky wondered
if he had forgotten how to talk.

"We aren't going to say that you *have* to go to the Bible
camp, Winky. But your mother and I feel that it is time
for you to be thinking seriously about Christian things,
and we know that you would like this camp very much.
Of course, there will be a lot of swimming, games, hiking
and other things that you like so well."

"You would still be able to spend a couple of weeks at
Grandfather's," Mom reminded. "Maybe," she looked at
Dad, "we would let you stay three weeks at Grandfather's
ranch."

"Maybe," Dad agreed. "Well, it's up to you, Winky. Perhaps you can decide and tell us by lunchtime."

Without saying a word, Winky stumbled away from the table. Dad always read from the Bible after breakfast, but this morning he didn't remind Winky to come back, because he wanted his son to have his mind free to make the important decision.

CHAPTER 2

As soon as Winky got outside, Boston came running to him. The little bulldog seemed to know whenever his young master was in trouble, and now he looked up at Winky with big round eyes. His pudgy nose sniffed the air inquisitively, and he seemed to say, "What's the matter, pal?"

"I'm having trouble, Boston," Winky said, as they strolled beside the hedge. He lay down on the grass beside the lily pool, and his faithful dog cuddled up close to him. "I tell you, Boston, I don't know what to do."

Boston whined.

"You know how I've been talking about going out to Grandpa's ranch, Boston? Remember last summer how you chased rabbits? And that one time you almost ran down a coyote? Sic 'em, coyote! Remember?"

Boston leaped to his feet and pricked up his ears.

"Mom and Dad want me to go to a Bible camp. 'Course, I know that's the right thing, and I guess I ought to like things about the Bible more. But Grandpa always reads the Bible at the breakfast table, like Dad does."

Winky's eyes began to twinkle. "Sure, Boston! That's kind of sort of almost pretty near just about like a Bible camp. Isn't it, Boston?"

Boston was watching a bumblebee that buzzed above one of the lily blossoms.

"Don't you think so, Boston?" Winky asked, almost expecting his dog to agree with him.

Boston yawned, and with a low grunt flopped down on his stomach and closed his eyes for a little cat-nap, though, of course, a dog can't really take a cat-nap because a dog isn't a cat.

Winky was sure that his dog was disagreeing with him.

"Of course," he continued, "Mom and Dad say I can go to the ranch after the Bible camp."

But Boston was asleep, so he didn't hear what his master was saying.

Winky rolled over on his back. Above him a great cloud was rolling across the sky. He saw how much higher it was from that cloud up to the blue above. Millions of miles, he had been told. Somewhere up there was God, he thought. And then he remembered that only last Sunday his Sunday school teacher had said, "God is right here with us, boys and girls, and He knows not only what we are doing, but He knows our thoughts."

God knows our thoughts! Winky hadn't really thought of it that way before. That must mean that yesterday at morning devotions when, instead of listening to the Bible reading, he was thinking about the ice cream cone he was going to buy with the nickle he earned carrying out Mr. Barton's ashes, God knew about it. Say, he was going to have to be more careful about his thoughts.

That meant he couldn't even think about whether he should go to the Bible camp or to the ranch without God's knowing about it.

It was nice of Dad to say that he could decide for himself whether or not he wanted to go to the camp. His parents could have said, "Now, Winky, we know what's best for you. We know that it will do you more good to go to the camp than to go to the ranch, so don't try to argue with us." But Mom and Dad weren't that way.

Well, then, that settled it. If they would let him do as he pleased, he would do what he wanted to do. He would go to the ranch! That might hurt Dad's and Mom's feelings. Boy, he didn't ever want to hurt Mom's feelings, or Dad's either.

He was so busy thinking that he didn't see his father's

shadow brush across Boston and then come up and touch
his own shadow.

"Thinking, Winky?" Dad asked in a kind voice.

"Wh—uh . . . Oh, I didn't see you, Dad!"

"I didn't mean to frighten you."

Winky stood, waking Boston, who went over to Mr.
Wilcox to be given the usual patting on his sleek back.

"I thought maybe I could help you decide how you're
going to spend your vacation."

"Oh," Winky mumbled.

"Your mother and I have been talking since you left
the house. We have decided that perhaps it will be best
for you to go to my father's ranch as we have planned."

"Oh, boy!" Winky almost jumped out of his shoes. "Do
you really mean that, Dad? I . . . I'll run all kinds of
errands for you, and I'll wash behind my ears before every
meal, and even before going to bed . . . and . . . and . . ."

Dad continued, "You see, Winky, your mother and I
are very anxious that you grow up to be a Christian."

Winky's eyes turned downward.

"But we wouldn't try to *force* you to become a Christian.
Even God won't do that. The Bible says, *Whosoever will,*
not *Everybody must,* when it invites us to accept Christ
as our Saviour. Do you understand what I'm trying to
tell you?"

Winky nodded.

"Well, you had better start getting your things packed,
because you'll be taking the train right after lunch Monday
afternoon."

Winky didn't know whether to be very glad . . . or
very sad . . . or just sort of in between.

CHAPTER 3

"Oh, boy, there comes the train!"

Boston, who had been placed in a big cage on the baggage truck, must have known what it meant for the *Rocky Mountain Limited* to come puffing into the station, because he gave a howl that almost made more noise than the whistle.

"Be sure you don't lose your ticket," his father warned.

Mom added, "Now, remember always to say *please* and *thank you*. And don't forget to help Grandpa and Grandma with the work whenever you can."

The big locomotive chugged by, and Winky was sure it winked at him out of the firebox, as if to say, "We're on our way to the Rockies!"

There was a tiny tear in Mom's eyes, and something hard stuck in Winky's throat. It made tears come to his eyes, too.

"Good-bye!" he waved.

"All aboard!" the conductor called, as he waved his arm to the engineer.

Toot! Toot!

Winky hurried to his seat, so he could wave from the window.

Choo! Choo! Choo! Choo!

"Good-bye!" he called so loudly that it awakened a cranky old man in the next seat.

There was the schoolhouse. There was the park. Now farmhouses began to dart past the window. As they rounded a curve, Winky could see the city limits from his window. Then the train followed the tracks beside a hill, and all that could be seen was country.

Winky hadn't been so excited since last spring when

he had his tonsils out, and then he had been excited because he was afraid instead of happy.

"Well, young fellow," the conductor, a plump little man with a big smile, said, "it looks like you're riding alone."

"Yep!" Winky grinned, and, of course, his eyes twinkled. "Do you want my ticket?"

"People usually have tickets when they get on my train," the conductor laughed.

Winky had a real billfold, and it had a shiny new one-dollar bill in it. He wondered how he would ever be able to spend so much money during just one summer, when he would be in the country away from soda fountains and candy cases.

"I've got my ticket in here," he told the conductor.

"Say, that's a nice billfold!"

"Yep, Mom gave it to me for Christmas."

"You must have a very nice mother."

"She's the nicest mom in America . . . in the whole world, I guess," Winky said.

When the conductor looked at the ticket, he chuckled, "You are taking a nice trip, aren't you? Foothills, Colorado! I used to work on a local train that went through Foothills. That was before I started to work on the *Limited*." He placed the ticket carefully in a yellow envelope. "I'll see to it that your ticket isn't lost, and I'll return it to you when we get to Denver." Then he wrote something on a slip of paper and placed it above Winky's window. "Have a nice time," he said, as he walked away.

The cranky old man in the next seat turned around and looked at Winky. Then he turned back again and tried to go to sleep.

Winky decided that he wasn't going to have any trouble with that man, and he was very glad when he got off a couple of stops down the road.

Most of the people in the coach were friendly. There

were some soldiers and sailors who stopped to pat Winky
on the head, and asked him if he was a good ball player,
and where he was going, and other things like that. A
lady across the aisle, who looked a lot like Grandma, gave
him a big apple and a candy bar.

"Thank you, ma'am," Winky said very politely.

There were farmers working in the fields, and boys and
girls were playing in the towns they passed. In one town
he saw a lake where people were swimming. He wondered
if the water in the brook where he and Bobby and Mike
and Donny went swimming would be as cold this summer
as it had been last summer.

When it began to get evening Winky grew tired of looking out of the window. Mom had made him a lunch. The
apple and candy bar had kept him from getting hungry
sooner, but as he opened his box and saw the sandwiches,
the fruit and the cake Mom had put in it, he was ready
for a big meal.

Darkness came very soon, and before long the lights were
turned out in the coach so that people could sleep.

But Winky couldn't sleep, for he began to think. He
wondered if he was running away from God. He almost
wished he would have decided to go to the Bible camp
instead of to the ranch. His heart felt very strange to-
night. It felt as if it had gotten very dirty and needed to
be scrubbed with a brush. *Wash me, and I shall be whiter
than snow. Though your sins be as scarlet, they shall be
as white as snow.* He had read those words in the Bible.

It was very dark outside. He couldn't see a thing. But
he knew God could see him. God knew that he didn't want
to go to the Bible camp. God knew that he was a sinner,
because if he was old enough to ride all alone on a train,
he was old enough to know that he needed to be saved.

"I wish I were a Christian," Winky told himself. "I
guess I should have gone to the Bible camp."

He tried to pray, but "Now I lay me down to sleep . . ." was all he could say. Winky knew that when you have sins to be forgiven, you must pray your own prayer, not a prayer somebody has made for you. But he couldn't pray. He was afraid God wouldn't hear him if he did pray, but he was wrong, for God *does* hear prayers, and He answers, too.

At last he fell asleep.

"Denver! Denver!" was the next thing he heard. Opening his eyes, he saw that it was morning.

"See the mountains, young man." The nice lady who had given him the apple and the candy bar pointed through the window.

"The Rockies!" Winky shouted. "Oh, boy! The Rockies!"

When they entered the depot, a negro porter came and took Winky's hand.

"That's your train over there. It leaves in ten minutes. Here's your ticket. Be sure you don't lose it."

"Hello, Boston!" Winky saw his dog being moved to the next train.

Boston tried to jump out of his box, and he must have flattened his nose a little more, though a bulldog's nose is about as flat as it can be.

"That your dog?" one of the baggage men asked.

"Yep. Could I pet him, just a minute?"

The baggage man lifted Winky long enough for him to stroke Boston's head. Boston kissed his master's hand about forty-seven times, and he whined when Winky walked away.

"We'll soon be there," Winky cheered.

Then he entered the train.

The railroad track followed the foothills nearly all of the way, and Winky did not once lose sight of the mountains. Even though he had seen them before, he couldn't stop looking at the beautiful snow-capped peaks.

Watching the mountains made the time pass rapidly, and before he expected it, the conductor of this train, who wasn't nearly so nice as the one on the *Limited,* said, "Foothills is the next stop, little boy. Be ready to get off."

Winky didn't like anybody to call him "little boy," but he was so excited that he hardly scowled a bit.

Just as the town loomed into view, the conductor came and helped him to the door.

The train squeaked to a stop, and Winky went down the steps.

"Hi, Winky!" Bobby, Mike, Annie, Donny and Lucy, who had come to greet him, shouted together.

Grandpa picked him up in his strong arms, and both he and Grandma kissed him.

"Hello, everybody!" he laughed.

"Did you bring Boston?" Mike asked. "Oh, there he is coming off the baggage car! See, gang? There's Boston!"

Quickly, they got Winky's things into Grandpa's car. They let Boston out of his box, so that he could run around the depot three or four times to exercise his tired legs. Then they started for Grandpa's house.

"You've really got a surprise waiting for you at the ranch!" Bobby said, as Grandpa shifted into high.

"What is it?" Winky asked eagerly.

Grandma smiled, "You could never guess, Winky."

"Tell me!" Winky begged.

"You'll find out in a few more minutes," Grandpa said.

And all the gang shouted, "And, boy, *will you be glad!*"

CHAPTER 4

Mike and Donny carried Winky's two suitcases to the ranch house. Winky followed them. He was sure that somewhere in the ranch house, a two-story frame building that stood right on the edge of the foothills beneath Snowcap Summit, was the surprise his grandparents had promised.

He didn't see that Bobby Anker, his very best pal, had sneaked away in another direction.

"Where's Bobby?" he asked as they were about to enter the house.

"Hmm," Grandpa's eyes sparkled, "I wonder where he could be?"

"Did he go home?" Annie teased.

Grandma gently pushed Winky's shoulder. "Into the house, Winky," she said.

Winky asked, "Is the surprise in there?"

"Oh, my," Grandma laughed, "I hope not!"

Grandpa agreed, "No, it would never do for you to bring your surprise into the ranch house, Winky."

Lucy giggled. "Wouldn't that be funny, if Winky brought his—"

"Lucy!" Donny, her brother, scolded.

"Oh!" Lucy held her hand tightly over her mouth. "I almost told!"

By this time Winky was so anxious he didn't know what to do. "You're sure it isn't in the house?" he asked, going into the parlor.

Lucy giggled again. "Positive!"

Through the western window, Winky got a glimpse of the Rockies, with Snowcap towering above the rest of the peaks.

"Boy, it's good to see the Rockies again," Winky said, for he tried not to let the others know how impatient he was to discover the surprise. "There's always snow on Snowcap, isn't there? Maybe can we try hiking up there this summer?"

"Ah," Annie teased, "Winky doesn't want to climb any mountains. He doesn't want to let on how anxious he is to find out about the secret."

Winky grinned, and everybody knew Annie was right.

"Say," Winky asked in another moment, "where did Donny and Mike go?"

"I wonder!" Lucy giggled.

Just then Fritz Ward, one of the ranch workers, came into the house. "Hello, Winky! Good to see you!"

"Hi, Fritz!" Winky forgot about the surprise for a while. "Where are Panhandle and Red?"

"Out rounding up a carload of steers to go into Denver in the morning."

"Boy, Fritz, I'm going to have to see that! Is that where Mike, Donny and Bobby are . . . waiting down at the corral?"

"They're down around there somewhere," Fritz laughed. "Why don't you help me put the steers in the corral, when Red and Panhandle bring up the herd?"

"He might get trampled on," Grandma said.

"He could ride one of the broncs, couldn't he?" Fritz winked.

"Wish I could ride a horse." Winky whined just a little. That was one thing about the ranch that disappointed him. All of the horses were much too wild for him to ride.

"Why not?" Fritz laughed. "You've got to learn sometime. I wasn't much older than you when my ranch boss down in Texas got me the prettiest little pinto that ever followed a canyon."

"But he never bucked, did he," Winky asked, "like Blackie, Dynamite, Flash and . . . and all the rest of Grandpa's riding horses?"

"Well," Fritz admitted, "he was a right gentle pinto."
A strange sound came from outside the kitchen door.
Winky asked excitedly, "Are the steers stampeding,
Fritz?"

But before Fritz could answer, Grandpa called from outside the kitchen door, "Your surprise is here, Winky!"

"My . . . My surprise? Oh, boy!"

In his rush to get to the door, Winky almost sent Fritz
sprawling.

And if ever those twinkling eyes of Winky's had twinkled,
it was now. Outside the kitchen door, Boston was eagerly
barking at the nicest present a boy on a ranch could ever
dream of receiving.

"See," Grandpa laughed, "even Boston likes the surprise!"

"A . . . A . . . Shetland p-pony," Winky gasped.

"All for you, Winky," Grandpa said. "Do you like him?"

"Oh . . . Oh, boy! I . . . I," Winky went to the pony
and stroked his soft brown and white neck, "sure do!"

The pony, who seemed to know that Winky was to be
his master, gently sniffed Winky's arm.

"See," Winky screamed, "he likes me! And look at his
saddle! Just like the cowboys ride in!"

Fritz pointed. "See, there comes the herd! Get into
the stirrups, Winky, and we'll join the round-up!"

Mike and Bobby helped him climb into the saddle. Winky
boldly grasped the lines.

"Giddap, Mustang!" he shouted. "Mustang! That's what
I'm going to call him! Mustang!"

Mustang broke into an eager trot, and before they were
halfway to the corral, Winky almost had a side-ache.

"Don't sit so stiff," Fritz, who was running along beside,
said. "Relax."

Little by little, Winky learned how to ride his pony, and
by the time the last of the steers were being driven into
the corral, he dared to urge Mustang into a slow gallop

and go out and round up one of the tired animals that had tried to run away.

Donny, Bobby, Lucy, Annie and Mike watched from the top railing of the corral. Of course, even Lucy and Annie knew how to ride, as they had lived on the ranch all of their lives. But they were surprised to see how rapidly Winky was learning to stay in the saddle. He hadn't fallen off even once!

"You ride like a real cowboy . . . almost," Bobby commented when Winky and Mustang, with Boston at their heels, pulled up to the corral gate.

And Winky's eyes twinkled when he heard that, you may be sure.

CHAPTER 5

The sun came up with a big smile on its face. Winky was only half through dreaming about eating an ice cream cone as big as the Empire State Building (that's the biggest building in the world, you know), but he jumped out of bed anyway.

"Well, look who's coming!" Grandpa exclaimed, when Winky came downstairs.

Grandma added, "I thought you would sleep until noon, after your long trip."

"I've got to learn to ride Mustang a little better," Winky beamed, as he hurried toward the door.

"Just a minute," Grandma called. "You can't go out without some breakfast."

"Aw, I'm not very hungry, Grandma."

"Now, Winky, no cowboy would ever ride the range on an empty stomach."

"Wouldn't he?"

"Of course not!"

"Then," Winky consented, "I guess I'll have a little breakfast."

"Wash your hands and face," Grandma said, "while I fry some bacon and eggs and make you some toast to go with a glass of cold milk."

Grandma had to scold Winky four times, or maybe it was five times, because he ate too fast. He almost ate an egg, a piece of toast and two strips of bacon in three bites when he happened to see Mustang through the window.

When he at last finished his breakfast, he ran out of the house toward the small horse corral near the barn. Boston followed him.

"Hi, Mustang! Remember me?"

Mustang stuck his nose through the corral gate. He shied back a little when he saw Boston.

"Don't be afraid of Boston, Mustang," Winky assured. "He's my pal, too."

Fritz and Panhandle came from the barn.

Panhandle said, "We'd better teach Winky how to saddle his pony, Fritz."

"Good idea," Fritz agreed.

Red came from the barn, his bushy crimson hair sticking out from beneath his ten-gallon hat.

"Bring the pony saddle, Red," Panhandle called.

"O. K.," Red said, as he turned back to the barn.

Panhandle and Fritz guided Mustang out of the corral. He was very gentle and didn't make any attempt to run away. First they saddled the pony, explaining each of the straps and buckles to Winky. Then they let him saddle the pony, because the saddle, though strong, was light enough for an eight-year-old boy to handle. And what do you suppose? The second time, Winky put on the saddle and bridle all by himself.

"Roll me up in a sleeping blanket full of spurs!" Panhandle exclaimed. "You sure learn fast, Winky!"

You know what Winky's eyes were doing as, crawling on Mustang's back, he said, "Boy, I know how to saddle my pony! I guess that's sort of wonderful!"

Winky rode all morning. He helped round up some stock that had strayed down the shallow canyon east of the corral. He saw his first rattlesnake of the summer during that gallop.

"Aw," Panhandle had drawled, "don't look so scared, Winky. Them rattlers is more fuss than danger. That's why they rattle. They don't want to be bothered."

Winky swallowed hard. He was afraid of rattlers.

"They bite, don't they?" he asked Panhandle.

"I ain't sayin' you should try to pet one of them fussy fellers on the head, like you would a kitten, but I do say don't be scared of 'em. They always let you know where they are. Stay out of their way, an' they'll keep out of your way, too."

Winky wasn't so afraid of the snakes after that, and when as they were bringing the cows back, another big fellow scolded at them, he watched the rattler without being afraid a bit.

Fritz said, "I've slept on the range right beside a prairie dog hole that a rattler had taken over for the night, and when he spotted me the next morning, he ducked his head back into the hole quicker than you can say Denver. But," he urged his horse into a trot after a cow that had spotted green buffalo grass off to one side, "like Panhandle says, don't try to make trouble with a rattler."

Winky was sure his stomach had grown to twice its usual size since he had come, for at noon he ate six potatoes . . . little ones, though . . . two helpings of diced carrots, a big piece of round steak (Grandma surely knew how to fry round steak!), two glasses of milk, three slices of bread and a big piece of apple pie.

He had just finished the pie when there was a knock at the door.

"Yes," Grandpa called, "who is it?"

"Mike and Bobby," Bobby called.

"Then why don't you come in?" Grandpa chuckled. "It's only strangers and folks who don't like us that knocks at this house. The rest walk right in."

"Hi, Winky," Bobby greeted.

"Hi," Mike added.

The three boys soon went outdoors.

"How do you like Mustang by now?" Mike asked.

"I've been riding him all morning."

Bobby laughed, "You'll be so stiff you won't be able to walk."

Winky rubbed his legs. "I guess I am kind of stiff."

Mike said, "We've got our swimming suits, Winky. Get

yours, too." Then he asked, "Shall we go over and swim at Donny's?"

Bobby said, "That's two miles. Pretty far to walk on such a hot day, isn't it?"

"We can all three ride Mustang," Winky said, "if we take off the saddle."

"Good idea!" Mike agreed.

They brought Mustang from the barn and removed his saddle. Then they led him to the corral wall where they could climb up on the rails and crawl onto his back. In another minute they were on their way. Boston followed them, as usual.

Donny was busy hoeing in the garden.

"Can't you play this afternoon, Donny?" Mike asked.

"I have to hoe up all these weeds first. I guess you'd better go ahead and play. I suppose you're going swimming."

"That's what we plan on," Bobby said. "Can't you come along?"

Donny leaned against his hoe. "I sure wish I could go along, but—"

Winky's eyes twinkled, "Why can't you?"

"I've got to hoe all these rows in the garden."

Winky said, "Hurry up and find three more hoes, and we'll all get to work."

"Sure!" Bobby and Mike agreed. "We'll all help!"

In less than half an hour, by helping each other, the boys had the weeds all hoed and were on their way to the brook for a swim.

CHAPTER 6

The water in the brook where they went swimming came from the snow melting around the timber line of Snowcap.

"Seems like the water would be warmer when it gets this far." Winky shivered.

Bobby laughed: "Oh, this isn't cold, Winky. Is it, Mike?"

Mike chattered, "N-n-o-t v-v-v-er-r-ry."

In the brook was an old-fashioned buggy partly covered by the water. The boys balanced themselves a moment on its highest wheel, then plunged headfirst into the water. Gradually, Winky got used to the cold brook.

After they had been swimming almost an hour, the boys sprawled out on the sand to sun themselves.

"Boy," Winky said, "Snowcap is so beautiful. We ought to take a hike up to at least the timber line this summer."

"You mean walk?" Donny asked.

"Sure, why not?"

"It's too far, Winky."

"How far?"

"It must be five miles to the foot of Snowcap," Bobby said.

"We can ride Mustang," Winky told the boys, as he pointed toward the Sutherland barn, where Mustang was at the moment enjoying a feast of alfalfa hay and corn.

Mike argued, "Mustang couldn't carry all of us, and, besides, Annie and Lucy would want to go along."

"Sure," Donny agreed, "we've got to have the girls along, so they can make the picnic sandwiches."

Winky was very busy thinking. It surely would be fun to take a trip into the mountains with the rest of the gang. There wouldn't be much driving by car to the mountains this summer, with gas rationing.

"We can hike around here in the foothills," Bobby said. "Some of them are kind of high."

All of a sudden an idea hit Winky right where he got all of his big ideas. Did his eyes twinkle! They almost turned somersaults right in his head! He rushed to the water.

"What's up, Winky?" Donny called.

"Come here," Winky shouted, "and help me pull this old buggy out of the water."

"What do you want it for?"

Winky told the fellows, "We're going to fix it up so we can hitch Mustang to it and take a trip to Snowcap!"

"Hey!" Bobby shouted. "That's a good idea, Winky!"

The buggy had mired deeply into the bottom of the brook, and the water from the mountain stream had washed even more dirt into its wheels.

"Uh," Winky grunted, "pull . . . fellows!"

"Wait a minute," Bobby told the gang. "Winky, let's you and I go into the water and lift on the wheels while Mike and Donny pull on the shafts."

Slowly but surely the buggy began to move.

"Pull!" Bobby urged.

"Uh! Uh! Whew! Uh! Uh!"

"Here she comes!" Winky laughed with glee as the buggy finally moved out of the brook.

"Say," Mike exclaimed, "this is a good buggy!"

Donny said, "I was afraid we might have to get some new wheels."

Bobby asked, "But you don't have any harness for Mustang, do you, Winky?"

"N-No."

"We've got to have a harness."

"Couldn't we make one?" Mike asked.

Donny suggested, "We've got lots of scrap leather in our barn. Daddy would let us have all we wanted. We've got a good riveting machine, too."

"It wouldn't need to be such a good harness," Bobby said.

"Come on, gang! Get on your clothes, and we'll pull the buggy up to Donny's place."

The buggy rolled easily over the ground, even when the boys had to go uphill, and they soon had it standing outside the Sutherland barn.

Mr. Sutherland came toward the boys, "What do you have there?"

"That old buggy that was down in the brook," Donny told his father. "We're going to fix it up so we can drive Winky's new pony."

"Say, now, that's a good idea!" Mr. Sutherland smiled.

"We don't have any harness for Mustang yet," Bobby said.

"We were kind of sort of wondering," Donny began, "if we could make a harness out of the old leather scraps in the saddle room of our barn."

"Hmmm." Mr. Sutherland thought a moment.

"We wouldn't take a bit more than we need," Donny said.

"Hmmm."

"Could we . . . maybe? Do you care, Daddy . . . very much?"

"No, I don't care."

"Oh, good!" Donny exclaimed.

"What's more," Mr. Sutherland continued, "I'll help you make the harness."

"Will you?" Winky shouted.

"I'm a little busy this afternoon, though. Could we start work on it tomorrow afternoon?"

"Sure! We'll all be here to help right after dinner tomorrow noon!"

CHAPTER 7

"Boston, come back here with that strap!" Winky scolded.
Nobody had played with Boston all afternoon, for everyone was busy helping Mr. Sutherland make Mustang's new harness.

Winky cornered Boston and, while the little bulldog growled and begged for a round of tag, he pulled the leather strap from Boston's mouth and hurried to give it to Mr. Sutherland.

"That strap will fit right in here," Mr. Sutherland said. "Maybe it ought to be shortened a couple of inches."

"Let us do that," Lucy offered.

"It looks like the girls are better harness makers than the boys," Mr. Sutherland laughed. "Maybe Mustang will think he's wearing a dress instead of a harness."

"Well," Annie said seriously, "Lucy and I are going to make a fly netting to go over his back."

Lucy broke in, "And we're going to make it cute, too."

"You know what I've been thinking?" Bobby said. "We ought to paint the buggy, so it would look better."

All of them nodded their heads.

Bobby continued, "We've got some white paint at our place that I know we can use."

"We could trim it with that red paint that was left over when Daddy painted the corral, couldn't we, Mike?" Annie asked her brother.

"Oh," Lucy clapped her hands, "red and white would be very nice, I think!"

Winky suggested, "Bobby, why don't you and Mike take Mustang and go get the paint? We can paint the buggy this afternoon, too."

"O. K.," Bobby agreed. "If we paint it this afternoon, it ought to be dry enough for the trip on Friday."

"Come on," Mike urged, walking to the stall where Mustang was tied, "and let's get going!"

"He'll want to gallop," Winky said, "because he's been tied so long. Be careful, though, so he doesn't get away and run back to Grandpa's."

"We won't let him get away," Bobby assured.

Away they went.

Those who stayed at Donny's house had helped add only a few more pieces to the harness, when the sound of hoofs came from up the road.

"They're coming back already," Donny said.

Winky smiled proudly. "Good old Mustang is no slow-poke!"

"I'll say he isn't," Annie agreed.

"Did you get the paint?" Lucy called.

"Sure we did!"

"Good!"

Mr. Sutherland said, "I'm almost as anxious to see Mustang hitched to a red and white buggy as you are."

"It's going to be beautiful!" Annie exclaimed.

Mr. Sutherland continued, "I'm almost through with the harness. Why don't you boys go ahead with the painting?"

"Sure," Lucy said, "you boys paint the buggy."

"O. K.," Winky agreed.

"We only brought two brushes though," Bobby said.

"I've got four or five good brushes over in our machine shed," Mr. Sutherland replied. "Go over and take what you need. You know where they are, Donny."

Donny brought the brushes, and after the paint had been well mixed, they began painting.

Bobby said, "The paint soaks right into the wood."

Mr. Sutherland told them, "The first coat always does that. You'll have to paint it once this afternoon and then paint it again tomorrow afternoon."

"Will it still be ready by Friday?" Donny asked.

"Things dry fast in this kind of weather," said Mr. Sutherland.

Before long it was time to go home. The harness was ready, and the buggy had been given one coat of paint. It still looked rather old and rickety, but Mr. Sutherland assured them that the second coat of paint would make it look almost new.

The next afternoon they were all back.

The second coat of paint went on as smoothly as butter. Mr. Sutherland was right. The buggy looked like new.

When they had put on the last bit of red trimming, Lucy and Annie exclaimed, "It's beautiful!"

Donny shouted, "I can hardly wait for Friday to come!"

Winky said, "We've got to have a name for our buggy."

"Sure," Bobby agreed, "we've got to have a name."

Mike laughed, "What could you ever call a buggy?"

Lucy, who always got good grades in school, smiled broadly as she suggested, "Let's call it *The Wonderful One-Horse Shay.*"

"That's a silly name," her brother Donny scolded.

"It is kind of funny," Mike said.

"Haven't you ever heard of *The Wonderful One-Horse Shay*?" Lucy asked. "It was a buggy that a man in a poem owned, and one day it fell apart all at once."

"I hope this buggy doesn't fall apart," Winky said.

"Of course it won't." Lucy was a little disgusted that no one laughed at her joke. "I was only fooling." She paused a moment. "Let's see . . . we could call it . . . no, that wouldn't be any good."

Mike suggested, "We could call it *Mustang's Buggy.*"

"Ah," Annie shrugged her shoulders, "that wouldn't be a good name."

"I know what!" Lucy brightened.

"What?"

"Let's call it *The Prairie Schooner!*"

"What's that?"

Lucy told them, "That's the name of a famous covered wagon."

"Is it?" her brother asked.

Winky agreed, "Sure, let's call it *The Prairie Schooner!*"

Mr. Sutherland spoke up. "I've got a whole box full of letters and numbers up in our attic. We used them to put the names over horses' stalls and other things like that. Why don't you go up and get the letters that spell *The Prairie Schooner*, Donny?"

"O. K." Donny ran immediately to the house.

Mr. Sutherland said to the others, "The letters are unpainted, but you can paint them red. That would look pretty nice, don't you think?"

"I'll say!" Winky smiled.

By the middle of the afternoon they had tried on Mustang's harness (it fitted perfectly), and the letters had been neatly nailed to the buggy. There was no doubt about it. *The Prairie Schooner* was good looking indeed.

CHAPTER 8

At last Friday morning came.

Winky heard the cow hands' alarm clock, which always rang a couple of minutes before Bantie, the rooster, began crowing, and when sleepy Panhandle reached over to turn off the alarm, Winky already had one stocking on. Through the window, as he dressed, he could see *The Prairie Schooner*. Mustang had pulled it home the afternoon before. The rising sun made its whiteness gleam and the red trimming glow.

It was agreed by the children and parents that the trip was to begin from the O'Grady ranch promptly at eight o'clock, and at eight o'clock, everybody was ready to go.

"Sure, an' ye be careful," plump Mrs. O'Grady warned.

"Don't worry," Mike assured.

Lucy emphasized, "We'll be all right, Mother."

Mike asked his father, "Don't you think Winky's pony looks dandy on the buggy?"

"Sure, and I guess he does," Mr. O'Grady agreed.

"O. K., Winky," Bobby urged, "let's get going!"

"Giddap, Mustang!" Winky shouted.

Mustang, with Boston at his side, jumped forward in a brisk trot, and the trip to Snowcap was on.

"Why can't Boston ride up here on *The Prairie Schooner* with us?" Annie suggested, after they had gone two miles and Boston had begun to look a bit tired.

"He can ride here," Lucy said, pointing to an old carpet they had brought with them.

"Sure!" Bobby said. "Let's let Boston ride. He can be the mascot of *The Prairie Schooner!*"

"What's a *maxskot?*" Donny asked.

Lucy laughed, "Bobby didn't say maxskot . . . he said *mascot.*"

"Oh, I see," Donny blushed. "A mascot is a bed where

a dog sleeps. That rug is Boston's cot . . . his mascot. Is that right?"

Everybody was laughing now, even Winky, who wasn't sure if he knew what a mascot was.

"Well," Donny pouted, "if a max . . . I mean mascot . . . if a mascot isn't a bed, what kind of a cot is it?"

Bobby informed, "A mascot is something . . . something that . . . well, it's something that—"

"See!" Donny clapped his hands. "Bobby doesn't know himself what a maxscot is!"

"Yes, I do," Bobby insisted. "A mascot is something that . . . that . . . that—"

"That what?" Donny teased.

Lucy came to Bobby's rescue. "A mascot is something that a team or some group of people chooses to be its special pet."

"Sure," Bobby shouted, "that's right! Don't you listen to the army-navy football game, Donny? The army has a mule for its mascot, and the navy has a goat, or something like that."

"And," Lucy added, "the Republicans have an elephant for their mascot."

"And," Bobby continued, "the Minnesota football team has a gopher, and Wisconsin has a badger, and—"

"Do they take elephants and mules and goats and gophers and badgers with them on trips like we take Boston?" Donny wondered.

"Well-l-l," Lucy admitted, "I guess maybe not."

"Then how come you say they're mascots?" Donny demanded.

"Anyway," Bobby insisted, "Boston is our mascot. Stop *The Prairie Schooner*, Winky, and we'll see if our new mascot wants to ride."

"O. K. Whoa, Mustang. Whoa, boy."

Mustang stopped obediently.

"Come on, Boston," the gang called in unison.

Boston looked up, surprised.

Winky said, "Up here, Boston. You can ride."

The bulldog came over beside the buggy and whined. Winky reached down and lifted him into *The Prairie Schooner*. He liked it, too. Of course, dogs can't really smile, but it did look as if Boston had a pleased grin on his face as they continued their trip.

"It isn't hard to see that God made the mountains," Lucy said.

"G-God?" Winky's eyes widened.

"God made the mountains!" Lucy emphasized.

"Of course He did!" Annie added.

Winky hadn't been thinking about God the last few days. He had been much too busy playing with Mustang and helping get *The Prairie Schooner* ready for the trip to Snowcap. God knew he was here. God knew that he didn't want to go to the Bible camp. God knew how funny it made him feel when he heard a minister or evangelist preach about sin . . . especially when the invitation was given at the close of the services.

He had heard how God judges those who try to run away from Him. Not many weeks ago the Sunday school lesson had been about Jonah. He wouldn't like to be punished like Jonah for trying to run away from God.

He wondered if God would punish him. Maybe God would let Mustang jump over a steep cliff and send buggy and all down hundreds of feet. No, God wouldn't do that. "God loves sinners," Mom had said, "and He wants them to be saved."

All of a sudden Winky wished ever so much that he were saved. But he wasn't. He knew that as surely as he knew his name was Winky.

"Maybe," he said to the others, "we ought to go back now."

"Go back?" Bobby exclaimed.

"Why do you want to go back?" Annie almost screamed. "It isn't noon yet, and we don't need to be back until night."

"Well," Winky's tongue stumbled, "I . . . I kinda, sorta . . . I . . ."

"It's not more than half a mile to the foot of Snowcap," Mike said. "Boy, it's going to be fun following the trail up the side of Snowcap for a few miles!"

"You don't really want to turn back, do you, Winky?" Donny questioned.

"N-No."

"Then why did you say we ought to go back now?" Annie asked.

"We won't go back," Winky said. "Giddap, Mustang. Let's go up to Snowcap."

In a few moments, the party reached the foot of Snowcap. Its rocky sides seemed to reach upward forever, and only when they stretched their heads back to their shoulders, could they see the white peak against the sea-blue sky.

They continued on for awhile. It became hard for Mustang to pull them, because the trail was steep. Then, too, men and animals tire easily in the thin mountain air.

When they came to a fork in the road, one leading to a wooded valley, the other on up the mountain, they stopped.

Lucy said, "Let's have our picnic dinner beside this mountain stream."

"Let's do!" the rest agreed.

Lucy said, as she stepped from *The Prairie Schooner* and reached for the picnic basket, "Mountain stream water is pure enough to drink, so we won't have to hunt for a spring."

"Sure," Bobby added, "you can drink mountain water. Do you know how the Indians used to drink?" He ran to the stream. "Like this. Look." He cupped his hands and dipped them into the water. "See. They filled their hands with water and then drank it like this." He lifted his hands to his mouth. "Awk!" he screamed. "Brrrr!"

Winky laughed with delight. "You poured the water all over you!"

Mike teased, "You'd better practice a little bit, Bobby."

"Aw," Bobby said, "that was an accident. See, I won't spill a drop this time." Once more he lifted water to his mouth, and once more he poured nearly all of the icy cold water down his neck. "Brrrrr! Whew, it's awfully cold! Whew!"

The others laughed so hard that if the mountains hadn't been so well fastened to the ground they would have tipped over . . . almost.

Lucy gave Bobby a cup after she had stopped laughing. "Drink out of this, Bobby."

"No, thanks," Bobby frowned, because he didn't like to have people make fun of him any more than you do, "I'm not very thirsty anyway."

For a few moments they watched the crystal clear water as it hurried down the mountain side.

"Look at the fish!" Winky exclaimed.

"We should have brought fish poles along," Donny said.

Lucy told them, "You aren't supposed to fish here. It's against the law."

"I guess so," her brother agreed.

"Let's get the lunch ready, Lucy."

"All right, Annie. You boys find a nice place where we can put the carpet that Boston sits on. Annie and I'll get things ready."

Soon the picnic lunch was spread.

Donny reached eagerly for a sandwich.

His sister scolded, "We must ask the blessing first!"

Donny blushed, "Aw, do we have to ask the blessing when we aren't home?"

"Of course!" Lucy insisted. "Shame on you!"

"Do you think we ought to ask the blessing, Winky?"

"S-Sure, Donny . . . I . . . I," Winky was thinking about God again, "I think we should always ask the blessing."

Lucy, who, like Annie, was a born-again Christian, was very pleased by what Winky said. She didn't know that he wasn't a Christian. If she had known that Winky hadn't asked for forgiveness for his sins and accepted the Lord Jesus Christ as his Saviour, as she and Annie had done, perhaps she wouldn't have said, "You ask the blessing, then, Winky."

"Uh . . . uh . . ." Winky stammered.

"Please," Annie begged.

Winky had been taught to pray, "God, bless this food, in Jesus' Name, Amen," but, strangely, he couldn't think of those simple words now. He wanted to *pray*, not simply repeat some words he had learned. He wanted to pray, *"God, be merciful to me, a sinner,"* like the man in the Bible.

"Please, Winky," Lucy prompted.

Awkwardly bowing his head, Winky prayed, "Dear Lord, . . . b-bless us, and bless this food . . . and . . . and help us to do what's right . . . and . . . and . . . lead us . . . to . . . to You. Amen."

"Amen," Lucy repeated reverently.

Annie slowly lifted her head; "Amen," she said.

Donny and Bobby and Mike stared strangely at Winky. They weren't making fun of his prayer, though he thought they were. They, too, were old enough to know that they, like Winky, needed to be saved.

CHAPTER 9

There wasn't a crumb left when Lucy and Annie put the plates back in the basket. It was the best picnic dinner either of them had ever eaten. Boston, too, was enjoying the chicken bones that had been tossed to him. Mustang had his fill of grass and a nibble of mountain fern for dessert.

"How do you feel, Mustang?" Bobby asked. "Do you think you can take us up a few more miles? It's downhill all the way back, you know."

"Here, Boston," Annie called, "your place is ready. Lift him in, Mike."

"There," Mike sighed, "how's that, Boston?"

Boston gratefully licked Mike's hand.

"He likes to ride," Donny said.

They climbed into *The Prairie Schooner*. Mike took the lines this time.

"Giddap, Mustang," he ordered, as he guided the pony up the trail.

"I wonder what time it is," Winky said, after they had ridden in silence for several minutes.

"Oh," Bobby looked up at the sun, "one-thirty, maybe two."

"Anyway," Donny added, "we won't need to start home for a long time."

"We've still got the picnic supper that Lucy brought," Annie reminded. "It's got two muskmelons in it, and some honey sandwiches."

Up, up, higher and higher they went. They let Mustang stop whenever he got tired and wanted to rest. He wasn't the least bit lazy, though, like some horses.

"Look!" Winky pointed downward. "We're up high!"

"I'll say," Bobby agreed.

"What's that road down there beneath us?" Winky asked.

Mike laughed, "That's the road we came on, Winky."
"Is it?"

"Sure, and see that road beneath it? We came over that trail, too."

"Really?"

"Honestly and truly, Winky," Mike said. He asked the others, "Didn't we?"

"Mike's telling the truth," they all assured.

"Boy," Winky exclaimed, "that's pretty far down there. And look at all the trees. L-Look!" Winky pointed. "What's that?"

"Where?" Bobby asked.

"Oh, I see what Winky sees!" Lucy pointed. "See, down by those big rocks? A herd of elk."

"Elk?" Winky asked. "Real, sure enough, live elk?"

"That's a herd of elk all right," they told him.

"Whoa, Mustang!"

Winky jumped out of *The Prairie Schooner* to have a better look. "See," he gasped, "they're coming this way! M-Maybe we'd better beat it!"

"Oh," the others scoffed, "they won't hurt us."

Bobby said, "As soon as they see us, they'll turn and run as fast as they can go."

"Are you sure they wouldn't hurt us?" Winky was doubtful.

"Not if you don't hurt them," Lucy spoke up. "Last fall a big elk almost killed a hunter, though, when the hunter wounded it."

"B-Boy," Winky shivered, "they're still coming this way!"

Then, suddenly, the leader of the herd stopped. He was a big creature with horns as thick as tree branches. He looked at them a moment, alarmed, and then, with an angry twist of his head, led the group in a fast gallop, so that they soon disappeared among the trees.

"See," Bobby said, "as soon as they spotted us, they ran away."

The party climbed into *The Prairie Schooner* and continued up the Snowcap Summit trail. Several times after that they saw herds of elk grazing. Once or twice they saw several mountain goats scampering from rock to rock high above them. By mid-afternoon the adventurers had reached a hut that was used as a ski camp in winter. It was here that they had their greatest thrill.

A dozen deer were sunning themselves on the bare ground outside the hut, while frisky chipmunks played nearby.

Winky had been the first to point to them. "Look! Deer!" And, as they approached, he said, surprised, "They don't run away."

"Maybe they're tame," Bobby suggested.

"Tame deer?" Winky was doubtful. "Up here in the wild country?"

"People who come up to ski probably feed them," Bobby said, "and that's why they're kind of tame."

"See," Lucy pointed, "there's where some hay has been left for them."

"And," Annie added, "that looks like grain of some kind spilled on the ground beside the hay scraps."

The deer seemed a bit alarmed as they approached, but though they cautiously moved backward, they seemed to have no thought of running away.

"Donny," Lucy told her brother, when they had stopped and were carefully getting out of *The Prairie Schooner,* "there are some sliced apples in our basket. Get some of them, and we'll see if we can get the deer to come and take the pieces out of our hands."

"Let Winky try first," Annie suggested, "because we've all done it before."

Sure enough, one of the deer slowly sniffed his way to

Winky and nibbled the sliced apple that he held in his hand.

"Oh, boy!" Winky was so thrilled. "Oh, boy! This is something wonderful! Oh, boy!"

They decided to have their picnic supper early, so they could eat it up here, for, though it was yet many, many miles before the trail reached the top of Snowcap, this was as far as they were going to go.

Once more Winky was asked to pray before they ate.

He didn't remember what he had said the moment after he had finished. A prickly feeling had come over him. It was loads of fun, this trip, but he was certain that he would be glad to give it up if he could be at the Bible camp. Somehow, he didn't feel safe up here. He felt that maybe something was going to happen to him, because he had tried to run away from God. He had never known before how serious a thing it is when a fellow does business with God about the salvation of his soul. He wasn't a very big sinner, he tried to do what was right, but the Bible said, *Ye must be born again . . . All have sinned, and come short of the glory of God . . . The wages of sin is death,* and he believed the Bible.

He only nibbled at the delicious lunch. "I'm not hungry," he said. He was too busy thinking to be hungry.

Maybe he was wrong, he tried to tell himself. Maybe God wasn't angry with him. God hadn't said He was angry with him for running away from the Bible camp. It was only that he felt that maybe God didn't like what he had done. Maybe it was all in his imagination.

And yet he wasn't sure.

"We'd better start toward home again," Bobby reminded, when the lunch was all gone. "It'll go faster down hill, but even if we make good time it'll be sundown by the time we reach home."

Mike stroked Mustang's soft neck. "All ready for another long trip, Mustang?"

Mustang rubbed Mike's shoulder with his pink nose.

"He's a dandy pony, Winky," Bobby said.

Winky didn't answer. He was stroking Boston's head, while he continued busily thinking.

"I say he's a nice pony, Winky," Bobby repeated.

Lucy laughed. "Winky thinks the mountains are so beautiful that he can't hear a word you say. Isn't that right, Winky?"

Winky nodded his head, though he didn't hear her question.

Mustang kept up a slow trot during the trip down. He didn't need to pull *The Prairie Schooner* at all. In fact, he had to hold back so it wouldn't go too fast.

Winky, who was driving, barely held the lines. Boston had crawled up into his master's lap and was asleep.

Donny said, "You've sure got it good, Winky. You've got Boston and Mustang. Boston's 'most near the best pup I ever saw, and Mustang is better'n any pony I ever saw."

"Maybe that's because Winky's a Christian," Lucy said. "God blesses Christians special."

Donny blushed, "Aw, that isn't it." Then he startled Winky by asking, "Are you *really* a Christian, Winky? Did . . . did you go forward at a meeting . . . and . . . and get prayed for?"

Winky felt small enough to crawl through a keyhole. He would have given a year's spending money if he could disappear all of a sudden.

"Are you, Winky?" Donny repeated.

A Christian? Lucy and Annie and the rest of the gang thought he was a Christian. But he knew he wasn't. What should he tell them? Should he lie, as he had once lied to his Sunday school teacher, and say that he *was* a Christian, even though he *wasn't*?

"Winky!" Bobby screamed. "A rattlesnake! Mustang, watch out!"

Everybody saw it, even Boston, who awakened with a start. Coiled at the side of the road, about to sink its ugly fangs into Mustang's leg, was a rattlesnake.

Just as the snake struck, Mustang, frightened by the warning rattle, kicked. His sharp hoof caught the viper squarely on the head and sent him sprawling across the ground. Then he broke into a furious gallop.

"Winky!" Bobby shouted, "Pull on the lines! Mustang's running away!"

"I can't!" Winky screamed. "I dropped the lines!"

"Help! Help!" Mike shrieked. "We'll be killed!"

"We'll go over the side of the mountain!" Donny moaned, wringing his hands.

CHAPTER 10

"Whoa, Mustang! Whoa, Mustang!"

All of them begged the frightened pony to stop, but it was no use. The rattle of *The Prairie Schooner*, as it bumped over the trail, hid their words from Mustang's ears. The buggy weaved from one side of the road to the other. Everybody was screaming for Mustang to stop. Boston, either because he was afraid or else because he liked the excitement, pointed his pudgy nose upward and howled.

"Look!" Bobby pointed. "That's where we had our picnic dinner! Mustang's taking the wrong trail home!"

"We'll be lost!" Mike added.

"Dear God," Lucy prayed loudly, "please help us! He'll help us, won't He, Winky?" she asked.

"Whoa, Mustang! Whoa!" Winky yelled.

"There's a storm coming!" Mike shouted after several minutes. Dark clouds were moving swiftly toward them.

In five minutes, the rain struck, and as it struck, Mustang, exhausted, stopped.

It wasn't like the usual rain, when one can see the drops. It was, rather, as though thousands of buckets of water were being poured at one time from the cloud above.

The rain refreshed Mustang, and he continued. The gang, huddled together in *The Prairie Schooner*, didn't know whether to stop him or let him go on, for they did not know how to get back to the main trail. The rushing torrents of water washed away their tracks as soon as they were made.

Poor Winky! He knew it was all his fault. He wanted to tell the others, to confess, but he was afraid. They might never be his friends again, if they knew that it was he who was to blame for their being lost.

The others tried to find protection from the fierce rain

storm, but Winky sat on the seat, letting himself become drenched. At least, he decided, he wasn't going to try to take up any room beneath the seat, the picnic baskets or the carpet, where the others were trying to protect themselves, though they were nearly as soaked by the rain as he.

The clouds didn't pass away, and when the rain settled down to a slow drizzle, it was already growing dark.

"Wh-What are we going to do, Winky?" Donny whispered, for he was frightened.

The others came out of their poor shelters.

"We can never find our way back," Bobby whined. "It seemed as if Mustang passed a fork in the road every half-mile. We'd never know which was the right road."

"I . . . I," Winky swallowed hard, "I don't k-know what we should do."

"We can trust God," Lucy reminded. "He knows where we are."

"Well, but . . ." Winky determined that he was going to confess to them. "I . . . I . . ."

"Oh," Lucy insisted, "don't say *but*, Winky. God really knows where we are! He takes extra-special care of us when we're sick or lost or in some other kind of trouble. The Bible says so. It says . . . it says . . . *Be careful for nothing; in every thing by prayer and supplication with thanksgiving let your requests be made known unto God.*"

Annie continued, "*And the peace of God, which passeth all understanding, shall keep your hearts and minds through Christ Jesus.*"

Peace! Winky wished he had peace!

"It's going to be awfully dark," Mike said.

Bobby added, "And it'll be dark in half an hour, almost, with those clouds. Maybe we'll be able to see for another hour."

"Anyway," Mike said, "we'd never be able to find our

way home." He fought back the tears. "I'd sure like to be home now!"

"I . . . I guess," Donny whimpered, "I guess we're *really* lost!"

"It's . . . it's," Winky tried again to confess that it was his fault, "it's . . ."

Lucy interrupted, "It's no use worrying, that's what. Don't you think we ought to stop Mustang and at least *try* to find our way back?"

Her brother said, "Mustang must have stepped on the lines when he ran away, because they're both gone."

"You can't drive a horse without lines," Mike emphasized.

"Maybe," Bobby suggested, "one of us could ride on Mustang's back and guide him that way."

Annie brightened. "I know what we can do!"

"What?"

"We can unravel part of this carpet and make two lines!"

"Good idea, Annie!"

Annie started immediately to loosen the long rag cords. from which the old carpet was made. She soon had two long pieces which would easily reach from Mustang's bridle to the driver's place on *The Prairie Schooner*.

"Whoa, Mustang!" Bobby called.

The pony, now over his fright, obeyed.

"I'll go out and fix the lines," Bobby offered. "Then we'll turn around and see if we can find our way back. Maybe we can."

"With God's help," Lucy added.

"Yes," Bobby admitted, "with God's help."

"Throw the line to me when you get it fastened," Mike told Bobby. "Tie it tight to the bridle. There won't be any more rattlers out, now that it's so much cooler after the rain, but we won't take any chances."

Bobby climbed back into the buggy. "Do you want to drive, Winky?"

"You drive, if you want to."

"O.K. What's the matter, Winky? Don't you feel very well?"

"I guess I'm all right."

Bobby turned Mustang completely around, and they began climbing again, in search of the road that led home. The mud was heavy now, sticking to the heels of the pony and the wheels of *The Prairie Schooner*, so they didn't travel very rapidly.

"It seems like we came from that direction," Bobby said, when they came to the first crossroad.

"Yes, see that overhanging rock?" Lucy pointed. "I remember it."

"Then we'll take that road," Bobby smiled. "Maybe it won't be so hard to find our way back after all."

"Only," Donny reminded, "it'll soon be dark, and we won't be able to see."

"Maybe, though," Mike cheered, "the clouds will clear and the moon will come out and we'll be able to see."

Mile by mile, inch by inch it seemed, they tried to find their way. Each time they came to a crosstrail, somebody thought he recognized a landmark that the party had passed before.

Little by little, Winky began to feel better. Nothing so terrible had happened. They didn't plunge down a steep cliff, as he had feared when Mustang began the runaway. No one was in the least hurt. They were lost, but they seemed to be finding their way back safely. Instead of being afraid, he had a feeling that maybe God was watching over him especially now, as He watched over real Christians like Lucy and Annie.

Down in his heart, where nobody but God could hear, he promised, "Dear God, if You will bring us safely out of the mountains, I promise that I'll give You my heart!"

He felt much better now.

"We'll soon be on the road home, maybe," he said to Bobby.

"Yep," Bobby chuckled, "and, boy, will that make me happy!"

"We wouldn't have been lost at all," Winky said, "if I hadn't dropped the lines."

"You couldn't help that," they all assured him.

"I got so scared when you yelled rattlesnake," he explained.

Lucy laughed, "Maybe Mustang didn't run away because of the rattler, Bobby. Maybe it was your yelling that frightened him so."

"Maybe," Bobby laughed. "I know I sure had goose pimples for a minute."

They rode on in silence for a few moments.

"It's cold having these wet clothes on," Donny said.

His sister added, "And they won't dry as long as it keeps on raining like this."

Winky asked, "How could a storm come like that, when there wasn't a cloud in the sky?"

"That's the way it is in the mountains. If we had had a car, so we could have gone up higher on Snowcap, we might have gotten above the storm."

"Above the storm?" Winky asked.

"Yes. You can see the clouds beneath you, even the lightning, and up where you are the sun is shining . . . kind of like being in an airplane."

"Whoa, Mustang!" Bobby called.

"What's the matter, Bobby?"

"We must not be on the right trail."

"Why not?"

Bobby explained, "Because here's another fork in the road, and both forks lead down again, not back up to where we lost the trail."

"That's right," Mike mumbled. "We came downhill all the way."

Once more fear made Winky's heart beat faster. They weren't safe yet. Maybe God would still send punishment. "Which way shall we go, Bobby?" he asked anxiously.

"I . . . I don't know, Winky."

"We're lost," Donny whimpered.

"And it's getting darker every minute," Mike said.

"Shall we turn around and go back, Winky?"

"Could we find the right trail if we did, Bobby?"

"I don't suppose."

Mike's teeth chattered, "We're going to spend the night in the mountains, and it's so cold with these wet clothes on."

"If it would stop raining," Lucy said, "it wouldn't be so bad."

At that moment there was a crack of thunder and the rain began to fall more heavily.

"Look!" Lucy pointed down the trail that led to the right. "Isn't that a house of some sort?"

"Where?"

"See, Winky, down there where the timber gets thicker?"

Bobby exclaimed, "I see it! It's a house all right! Giddap, Mustang, we're going to get out of the rain!"

CHAPTER 11

Night came before they had time to make out the nature
of their surroundings, except to assure themselves that
nobody lived in the deserted mountain cabin they had
found. The floors were creaky, and from various parts of
the roof steady streams of water leaked through.

"I wonder who ever lived here, Winky."

"I don't know, Lucy."

Bobby said, "Maybe some trapper lived here."

Mike argued, "But there's no trapping done in this part
of the mountains. This is a game refuge."

"Maybe the cabin has been here for many years."

"That's possible, Bobby," Mike agreed.

"Anyway," Lucy sighed, "it's a shelter. God led us here.
I know that."

"There's a fireplace," Donny said.

"But how could we ever make a fire?" Lucy asked.

"And if we did have any matches, what would we use
for fuel?" Annie questioned. "Any wood outside is soaked."

"We could tear up part of the floor," Donny said.

His sister told him, "What good does it do to talk? We
can't have any fire, that's certain. I'm glad we have a
shelter, and it's much warmer in here than outside."

"I'll say it is," Mike said. "I was getting pretty cold out
there in the storm."

"Listen to it beat on the roof! It's pouring again!"

"Say," Bobby said, "what about Mustang? Boston's in
here, but we left Mustang tied out in the rain."

"Let's take him in here," Mike said.

"Sure, we've got to get him in out of the storm."

Winky went toward the door.

Mike, Bobby and Donny quickly offered, "We'll go along."

Outside, Bobby said, "I tied him over here, I think. It
was by . . . Fellows! He's gone!"

"Gone?" Winky screamed. "Mustang!"

"Buggy and all."

"Are you sure you tied him, Bobby?"

"I thought so, Winky. I thought . . . maybe, though . . . maybe . . . I . . . I guess maybe I didn't tie him."

"Mustang! Mustang!" Winky called.

Lucy put her head outside. "Is Mustang gone?"

Donny said, "He must be. He was here when we went in."

Winky moaned, "Oh, he might fall down a steep bank during the night and . . . and . . . and be killed!"

A sharp streak of lightning filled the mountains with a moment of daylight.

"Did you see him anywhere?" Winky pleaded.

"N-No," Bobby admitted, "I didn't."

Now it thundered, and they couldn't speak for a moment. Winky determined, "I've got to find my pony." He walked away. "Mustang! Mustang! Where are you?"

"Winky!" Bobby begged. "Come back! You'll be lost in the storm!"

In the distance, through the falling rain, they heard Winky calling, "Mustang! Mustang! Where are you, Mustang? Please answer me, Mustang! Please come to me, Mustang!"

"Come on, fellows," Bobby told Mike and Donny, "we've got to bring Winky back."

Lucy warned from the door, "But you won't be able to find your way back either."

Annie said, "You'd better come in."

"I guess we'd better," Donny said meekly.

"And leave Winky out alone?" Bobby exclaimed. "We can't do that!"

"Mustang!" Winky's voice was farther away. "Mustang, where are you? Don't you hear me, Mustang! Don't you . . . Oh, help! Help! Help! I'm falling! Help!"

Then lightning flashed, thunder crashed, and they heard no more.

Bobby gasped, "He . . . Winky . . . must have fallen over a . . . a cliff!"

"Oh," Lucy cried, "how terrible!"

"Are you sure?" Annie asked.

Both of the girls joined the boys. Boston, too, came out of the house. He seemed very excited, for he noticed that Winky was missing.

"We've *got* to find him!" Bobby insisted.

There was more lightning and thunder, and another downpour of rain forced them to take shelter in the house.

*   *   *   *   *

Winky didn't know how long he lay at the bottom of the ten-foot precipice over which he had stumbled. When the rain let up a bit he began to regain consciousness. There was an ache in his head, where he had struck it during the fall. The mud into which he had fallen was soft, and for a moment, he thought he was snug in bed. But, as his mind became more clear, he remembered all that had happened.

Then, through the patter of the rain, he thought he heard singing. It frightened him, for who would be singing up here in this forlorn part of the Rockies? The singing became louder. It was the sound of many voices singing *The Old Rugged Cross*.

Winky tried to sit up, but the pain in his head made him fall back. He fainted again.

When he once more regained consciousness, he heard more singing. Hundreds of voices, somewhere in the distance, were singing *Jesus Saves*.

"Mom! Grandma!" Winky screamed. "I'm afraid! I . . . I'm dying! I . . . I hear . . . angels!"

The rain burst forth in all its fury now, and the singing faded away.

Maybe he only thought he had heard music. He remembered being told that when one is lost he thinks he hears many things. Then, too, it might have been the hard blow on his head that caused him to imagine he heard voices singing hymns.

*   *   *   *   *

In the cottage a few moments later, Bobby said, "The rain has let up again. We've got to try to find Winky."

"But how?" Mike asked.

Lucy burst forth, "I've got an idea!"

"What?"

"Why not let Boston find him?"

"Say, Lucy, that's a dandy idea!"

Annie warned, "But be sure you have him tied, so he can't get away."

"What could we fasten to his collar?"

Lucy suggested, "I've got what's left of that carpet, Bobby."

"Just the thing, Lucy!"

In a moment, the boys were ready to go.

"Look!" Lucy pointed through an open window. "The clouds are clearing! The moon is coming out! Thank You, Jesus!"

"We'll be able to see!"

The boys scampered out of the door, eager to find their lost friend.

Bobby said, "Find Winky, Boston! Find him, boy! Find him!"

"Wurruff! Wurruff!"

"See," Donny thrilled, "he's starting in the direction Winky went!"

By the light of the moon they could see where they were walking, and so they let Boston run.

"He's heading for that steep incline over there," Mike

said. "Maybe that's a deep canyon that Winky fell into."

"I hope it isn't too deep!"

"No," Donny said, "it isn't very deep, Bobby. See, there's water running down at the bottom."

They stopped at the edge of the bank. A low moan came up from below.

"Winky!" Bobby called. "Is that you?"

"H-Help!" Winky's voice came back in answer.

"It's Winky, all right," Bobby shouted. "We're coming, Winky!"

When they reached Winky, he had fainted again. Tenderly, the three boys picked him up and carried him up the steep bank to the shack.

Lucy shouted, "Oh, you did find him! We prayed that you would!"

Annie held her hand over her mouth. "Is . . . Is . . . Is he . . ."

"He's hurt pretty bad," Bobby informed.

"He's got a big cut on his head," Mike said.

Donny added, "We've got to get him to a doctor."

"A doctor," Mike asked. "How?"

"I don't know," Bobby cried.

"With God all things are possible," Lucy said.

"Could . . ." the moon filled Bobby's big blue eyes with light, "G-God send us a doctor way up here in the mountains?"

"God can do anything for those who are in need," Lucy said.

"Will . . ." Bobby fought back the tears, as he looked down at the silent form of his very best pal, "would . . . could you kinda pray for him now . . . awfully hard . . . and . . . and ask God to send us a doctor?"

Lucy dropped to her knees, folded her hands and turned her pretty face toward heaven. "Dear God, we need help.

We think Winky needs a doctor. If he does, dear God, please send one. In Jesus' Name. Amen."

"Amen," the others repeated after her.

CHAPTER 12

"You're all right," Bobby stroked Winky's feverish face when he began to regain consciousness half an hour later.

"Am . . . Am . . . Where . . ."

"You're back in the cabin, Winky."

"Cabin? Oh . . . I . . . I thought I had . . . d-died."

"You aren't going to die, Winky," Bobby assured. "You had a bad tumble, but you'll be O. K."

"I . . . I heard angels . . . singing," Winky mumbled.

The others looked at each other with wide eyes.

"He's out of his head," Donny whispered.

"I . . . I think they were angels," Winky continued. "I heard . . . them . . . singing . . . they were singing *The Old Rugged Cross,* and," he stopped for breath, "and *Jesus Saves.*"

"Take it easy, Winky," Bobby told his pal. "Don't try to move around too much. Does your head still hurt?"

"A little. Wh-Where's Mustang?"

"He'll be O. K., Winky."

"Sure he will," Mike emphasized.

"D-Did you hear the . . . angels?"

"You didn't really hear singing, Winky." Bobby stroked his face again. "You must have thought you did, after that hard bump on your head."

"M-Maybe," Winky muttered, as his voice grew weaker, "I j-just . . . th-thought I . . . heard . . . an-gels. Hundreds of them . . . thousands."

He lost consciousness once more.

"That's strange," Lucy said.

"He must have bumped his head awfully hard," Annie said thoughtfully.

Donny gulped, "D-Do g-ghosts sing hymns?"

"Donny!" Lucy scolded her brother.

"G-Ghosts, D-Donny?" Mike gasped.

"I . . . I sort of w-wondered."

"Well," Lucy scoffed, "stop such silly wondering. How could there be singing here in the mountains?"

Annie suggested, "Maybe there is someone around here whom Winky heard singing. There might be more cabins around here. Maybe there are better cabins that people live in."

Mike agreed, "Maybe, Lucy."

"But," Bobby said, "Winky told us he thought he heard hundreds of voices."

"That's right," Mike remembered.

"D-Do," Donny squirmed, "g-ghosts travel in b-bunches?"

"Donny!" Lucy shouted. "There *aren't* any ghosts! You know better than that!"

"I-I'm sc-scared!" Donny admitted.

"Silly, what of?"

"Ma be there are ghosts, Lucy. You don't know. Maybe Winky *did* hear ghosts singing."

"Sh!" Bobby warned. "Winky's stirring again! Don't talk about ghosts! We don't want to frighten him!"

"Did . . . you . . . hear . . . the singing?" Winky asked once more. "I heard . . . singing. Angels, m-maybe . . . hundreds of angels, maybe. It was pretty singing. They sang *The Old Rugged Cross* and—" Winky stopped. He sat up.

Bobby gently pushed him down again. "Careful, Winky! Careful!"

"I hear them again! I hear the angels singing! Oh, dear God, I'm sorry for my sins! Really I am!"

"You don't hear any singing, Winky!" Bobby said.

Lucy gasped. "Sh! Bobby! W-Winky *does* hear singing!" They all became silent.

From somewhere in the distance came the words:

> *Just as I am, without one plea,*
> *But that Thy blood was shed for me,*

And that Thou bidd'st me come to Thee,
O Lamb of God, I come! I come!

Just as I am, and waiting not
To rid my soul of one dark blot . . .

"Lucy," Annie grasped Lucy's arm, "wh-what is it?"

Winky was sobbing, "Dear God . . . I . . . I'm sorry I ran away! Dear God! Please help me! Please! *P-l-e-a-s-e!*"

Once more, he lost consciousness.

Those in the mountain shack heard the rest of the song. They had never heard such beautiful singing.

"It *m-must* be angels," Bobby stammered.

"Oh, I-I'm afraid!" Donny admitted. "I'm awfully afraid!"

"That's because you're not ready to meet God, Donny! That's why you're afraid!"

Mike and Bobby didn't admit that they were afraid, but they knew that Lucy was right. It was because they hadn't asked God to forgive their sins. They hadn't accepted Christ as their Saviour.

They didn't hear any more singing after that, but none of them tried to argue as to whether or not there really had been singing.

"Do angels come down to earth and sing?" Annie asked Lucy.

"I don't know."

"Do you think maybe those *were* angels?"

"I don't know, Annie," was all that Lucy could say.

All were quiet for several minutes.

"Maybe we'd better all try to sleep," Bobby suggested.

Mike said, "But I thought . . . I thought a doctor was coming."

"Do you think Winky needs a doctor?" Lucy asked.

Bobby answered, "There's a deep cut on his head, and I think it's still bleeding some. It would be awfully nice if a doctor would come."

"Well," Lucy was certain, "if Winky needs a doctor, God will send one."

No one spoke for almost half an hour.

It was Donny who gasped, "L-Listen! Th-There's somebody out-s-s-side the cabin! H-H-H-Help!"

Lucy whispered, "Sh!"

Annie said softly, "Someone's talking."

"I hear them too," Bobby whispered.

They became breathlessly silent.

A man's voice was heard outside the door. "I thought sure I heard a cry from in here."

The door was pushed open and the beam of a flashlight searched the inside of the cabin.

"Oh!" Donny screamed. "Don't hurt us! We didn't do anything!"

"Here they are, Doctor. In here."

"D-Doctor?" Lucy gasped. "God sent us a doctor!"

A friendly voice asked, "How on earth did you children get here?"

"W-We," Bobby tried to speak "w-were . . . on . . . on . . ."

"Don't be afraid. Is one of your number hurt?"

"Winky is," Donny said. "His head's hurt bad. Are you a doctor? My sister prayed that G-God would send a doctor."

The friendly voice chuckled, "Well, now, that surely proves that God answers prayer. Yes, we have a doctor here. Come on in, Doctor. There's a little fellow on the floor here who has been hurt."

Bobby said, "He fell and bumped his head."

The doctor, a young man, asked, "Give me your flashlight, George." He flashed it into the open wound on Winky's head. "Hmmm. Bad gash, all right, but it doesn't look serious. We'd better get all of these children over to the camp."

CHAPTER 13

The doctor gave Winky some medicine that kept him asleep until the sun came up the next morning. When he awoke, Lucy, Annie, Bobby, Mike and Donny were beside his bed. They were dressed in clean dry clothing.

"Wh-Where am I?"

"At a Bible camp," Bobby told him.

"B-Bible camp?" Winky gasped. "A camp for boys and girls?"

"How did you know?" Lucy asked him. "It's for grown-ups, too. There are hundreds of people here."

"Is . . . it L-Lake Mirror?"

"Lake Mirror?" Bobby questioned. "No, we're still in the mountains."

The doctor entered the warm cabin. "How's the sick boy this morning. Well, your face is a little brighter! That's a good sign!"

"H-How . . . Wh-What . . ." Winky was too puzzled to finish the question.

"Haven't you told him what happened?" the doctor asked Bobby.

"He just woke up, sir," Bobby answered.

"You're a very fortunate boy, Winky," the doctor said, for the gang had told him Winky's name. "I'm afraid it might have been too bad if you had fallen any other place in the mountains."

Bobby began to explain, "When Mustang ran away, Winky, and we got lost, it worked out that we came right to the edge of the big Rocky Mountain Bible Camp."

"Bible camp," Winky mumbled. "Bible camp."

"That dandy pony of yours," the doctor continued, "strayed down to the tabernacle, and when we saw him after the evening evangelistic service, we knew something was wrong, so we set out to look for you!"

"Th-Then I d-did hear singing!"

"Yes, Winky," the doctor chuckled, "these friends of yours tell me you thought you heard angels singing. You heard a thousand people here at the camp trying to sing above the noise of the rain on the tabernacle roof."

The door of the cabin opened. Grandpa and Grandma entered.

Grandma rushed to Winky's side. "How are you, Winky dear?"

"G-Grandma!" Winky gasped. "G-Grandpa!"

Grandma and Grandpa had been called by telephone.

"He's getting along fine," the doctor assured Grandma. "He'll be able to be up by tomorrow afternoon . . . in time for the big Sunday afternoon children's meeting."

"Ch-Ch," Winky choked, "children's camp!"

"What's the matter, Winky?" Grandma asked.

Winky began to cry—something that he very seldom did —but even the strongest people cry when they repent of their sins. "I . . . I've been r-running away from God."

"Winky, what are you saying?"

"M-Mom and Dad wanted me to go to L-Lake Mirror . . . to the children's camp there . . . but . . . but I wanted to come to the ranch. I knew God wanted me to get saved, but I tried to hide from God."

"Winky!" Grandma exclaimed.

"God made Mustang run away so I'd get to *this* Bible camp," Winky continued. "I want to be saved, Grandma! I want to be a Christian! I don't want to run away from God any more!"

The doctor laid aside his medicine kit and took a New Testament from his pocket. He was a Christian doctor hired to take care of the medical needs of this big conference.

He knelt beside Winky's cot.

"Shall we look into the Word of God, Winky?"

Winky nodded. As he looked up, he saw that there were anxious tears in the eyes of Bobby, Donny and Mike. So he said, "Maybe they'd like to be saved, too."

Immediately, the three boys knelt beside the doctor. Lucy, Annie, Grandpa and Grandma knelt, too.

"Believe on the Lord Jesus Christ, and thou shalt be saved . . . But as many as received him, to them gave he power to become the sons of God, even to them that believe on his name . . . Him that cometh unto me I will in no wise cast out . . ." The doctor read these and other verses on salvation to Winky and the other three boys.

"Now, fellows," he finished, "do you want to be saved?"

Winky's eyes twinkled more than they ever had, and the other fellows nodded their heads.

"You believe that Christ died for your sins?"

Yes, they believed that!

"Do you accept Him as your Saviour?"

One by one the boys prayed, as each of them invited the Lord Jesus Christ into his heart.

"I'm saved!" Winky cried for joy. "Grandma! Grandpa! Boston! Mustang! I'm saved!"

And how his eyes did twinkle!

Grandma said to the doctor, "God *did* lead our grandson to this Bible camp."

"I'm never going to run away from God again," Winky told them. "I'm going to be a real Christian, like Annie and Lucy." He pointed to the other three. "Aren't we, fellows?"

"We sure are!" Bobby and Donny and Mike exclaimed in unison.

"Yes, sir, Winky," the doctor spoke again, "you're going to be a happy boy when you get up. Your other playmates are already enjoying the children's camp. By the way, Winky, why don't you give your testimony at the camp tomorrow afternoon?"

"May I have Mustang with me? He took us here!"

"You surely may, Winky!"

"Good old Mustang! I'm glad he didn't get hurt!"

"He's as good as ever," Grandpa assured.

"Boy," Winky shouted, "won't Mom and Dad be happy when I write and tell them I'm a Christian? They've been praying lots for me! God really answers prayer!"

"He surely does!" everyone in the room agreed.

Printed in the United States of America